Adapted by Arie Kaplan

Based on the film *Despicable Me*

Illustrated by Elsa Chang

 A GOLDEN BOOK • NEW YORK

© 2019 Universal City Studios LLC. All Rights Reserved. Published in the United States by Golden Books, an imprint of Random House Children's Books, a division of Penguin Random House LLC, 1745 Broadway, New York, NY 10019, and in Canada by Penguin Random House Canada Limited, Toronto. Golden Books, A Golden Book, A Little Golden Book, the G colophon, and the distinctive gold spine are registered trademarks of Penguin Random House LLC. rhcbooks.com

Educators and librarians, for a variety of teaching tools, visit us at RHTeachersLibrarians.com
ISBN 978-1-5247-7163-8 (trade) — ISBN 978-1-5247-7164-5 (ebook)
Printed in the United States of America
10 9 8 7 6 5 4 3 2 1

Gru was a **super-villain**. But what he really wanted was to be the world's **GREATEST super-villain**. He decided to steal the moon!

Gru needed to make the moon small enough to steal. Along with his helpers, the Minions, and his friend Dr. Nefario, Gru planned to steal a shrink ray.

But they were outsmarted by another villain named Vector.

Now Gru would have to get into Vector's super-secure fortress.

BUT HOW?

Gru watched as three little girls rang Vector's doorbell.
They were selling cookies to raise money for the orphanage
where they lived. To Gru's surprise, Vector welcomed them in.
That gave Gru a brilliant idea!

Gru adopted the three girls, who were named
Margo, Edith, and Agnes. The orphans were happy to
have a home. They loved Gru and his funny Minions.

Gru took care of them and read them stories.
The villain didn't want to admit it, but he was starting
to enjoy being a dad.

"This is literature?" Gru exclaimed.

Soon it was time for the girls to deliver the cookies that Vector had ordered. But Gru had replaced the regular cookies with cookie robots. He couldn't wait to get that shrink ray!

"Girls, let's go!" said Gru.

The girls insisted on going to dance class first. Agnes gave Gru a ticket to their recital. He said he would go.

"Pinkie promise?" she asked.

Gru nodded. "Yes, my pinkie promises."

It wasn't exactly easy, but Gru and the Minions were able to get the shrink ray!

Now that Gru had the shrink ray, he could take the girls to **Super Silly Fun Land**, where they had been begging to go.

Gru helped Agnes win a stuffed unicorn.
"It's so fluffy!" she gushed.
Gru realized he loved the girls. They had become his family.

Gru also realized that the day he planned to steal the moon was the same day as the dance recital! Gru wanted to go to the recital . . .

. . . but he also *really* wanted to steal the moon.
Gru decided to steal the moon *very quickly*.
Then he could go to the recital, too!

Gru stole the moon just as he had planned. But when he got
to the recital, the girls were gone. Vector had captured them!
The villain would only free the girls if Gru gave him the moon.

So Gru gave it to him. But Vector didn't let the girls go.
Instead, he attacked Gru with missiles . . . and a shark! Gru
dodged them all. He was determined to get the girls back.

Now Vector was scared of Gru. He got into his flying machine and took off with the girls. Gru climbed onto the ship and held on tight, but he began to slip. . . .

As he fell, Dr. Nefario and the Minions
came to his rescue!

Just then, the shrink ray's power *wore off.*
Uh-oh! The moon began to grow *bigger and
bigger*! Vector held on to the moon as it flew
back up into the sky.

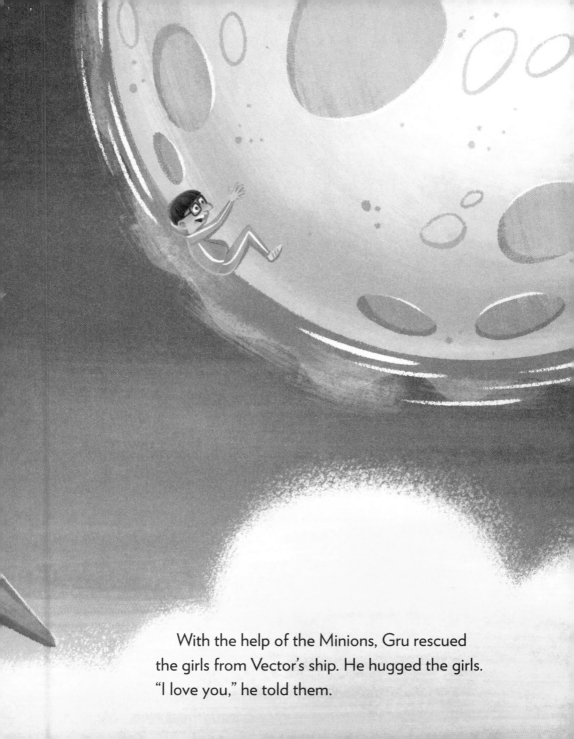

With the help of the Minions, Gru rescued the girls from Vector's ship. He hugged the girls. "I love you," he told them.

The moon was back where it belonged.
Gru didn't get to be the number-one super-villain,
but that was okay. He got something better.
He got to be a dad.